COVER

Timeless Tales

POEMS OF CHILDHOOD

Timeless Tales

POEMS OF CHILDHOOD

VOLUME ONE

BY E.V. EKLUND

Published by Waldorf Publishing
2140 Hall Johnson Road
#102-345
Grapevine, Texas 76051
www.WaldorfPublishing.com

Timeless Tales

ISBN: 978-1-68419-264-9
Library of Congress Control Number: 2016957049

AUTHOR   **ARTIST**
E.V. Eklund   E.V. Eklund

Dedicated
to
Mary & Rod Hoioos

Special thanks to my husband Abhay for
helping me make this book possible.

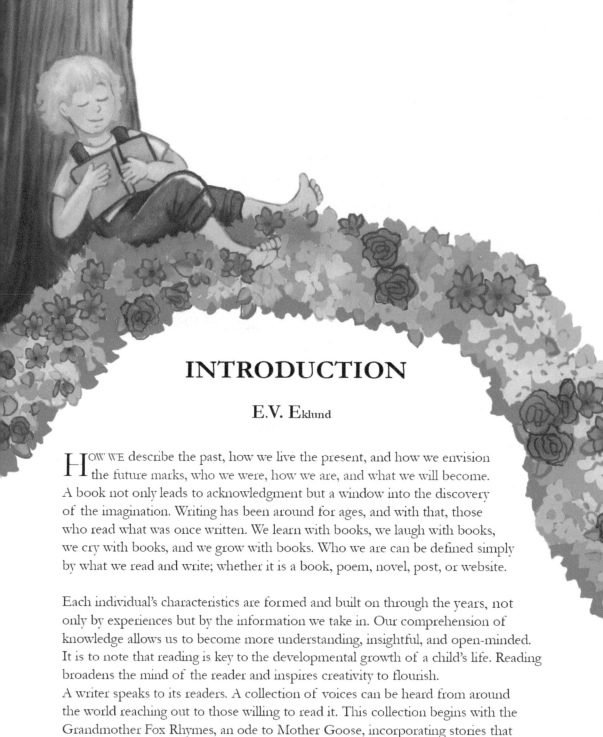

INTRODUCTION

E.V. Eklund

How we describe the past, how we live the present, and how we envision the future marks, who we were, how we are, and what we will become. A book not only leads to acknowledgment but a window into the discovery of the imagination. Writing has been around for ages, and with that, those who read what was once written. We learn with books, we laugh with books, we cry with books, and we grow with books. Who we are can be defined simply by what we read and write; whether it is a book, poem, novel, post, or website.

Each individual's characteristics are formed and built on through the years, not only by experiences but by the information we take in. Our comprehension of knowledge allows us to become more understanding, insightful, and open-minded. It is to note that reading is key to the developmental growth of a child's life. Reading broadens the mind of the reader and inspires creativity to flourish.
A writer speaks to its readers. A collection of voices can be heard from around the world reaching out to those willing to read it. This collection begins with the Grandmother Fox Rhymes, an ode to Mother Goose, incorporating stories that are their own. A key opens the door to the imagination of fairies and wizards, far away lands and dreams.

Poetry speaks to me now as it did when I was a little girl. My grandmother would have us sit down and read to us from a collection of classic poems called Childcraft: Poems of Early Childhood Vol. I & II by J. Morris Jones (Editor), Milo Winter (Art Director), and various authors and artists. A collection of different poets and artists together to create a world of wonder for young and old readers alike. This was my inspiration. To create, in a way, a Vol. III, and perhaps Vol. IV, rendition of the books I loved so dearly. Though I am but one voice and may, in no way, measure up to the classics we so love; I hope that you may find joy and pleasure with this collection. Perhaps some may even become a classic with your family to be read to your children and their children's children.

The imagination is essential in childhood. It is where we go to escape the harshness of reality and find solutions to problems. Children associate with rhythmic language, patterns and the elite form of expressionism presented in the form of poetry. This is what justifies the love children have for it.

When their imagination grows do they continue to seek the truth, a readiness for learning facts from fiction. The child now reaches for history, science, and society, as told in their own story.

I write to inspire, for your delight, memories of the past, of youth, and of the simple pleasures in life. My wish to you, my readers, is that you may find happiness. I introduce you to new memories and, perhaps, spark the forgotten ones of your childhood.

CONTENTS

GRANDMOTHER FOX NURSERY RHYMES

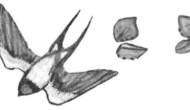

THE WORLD OUTSIDE

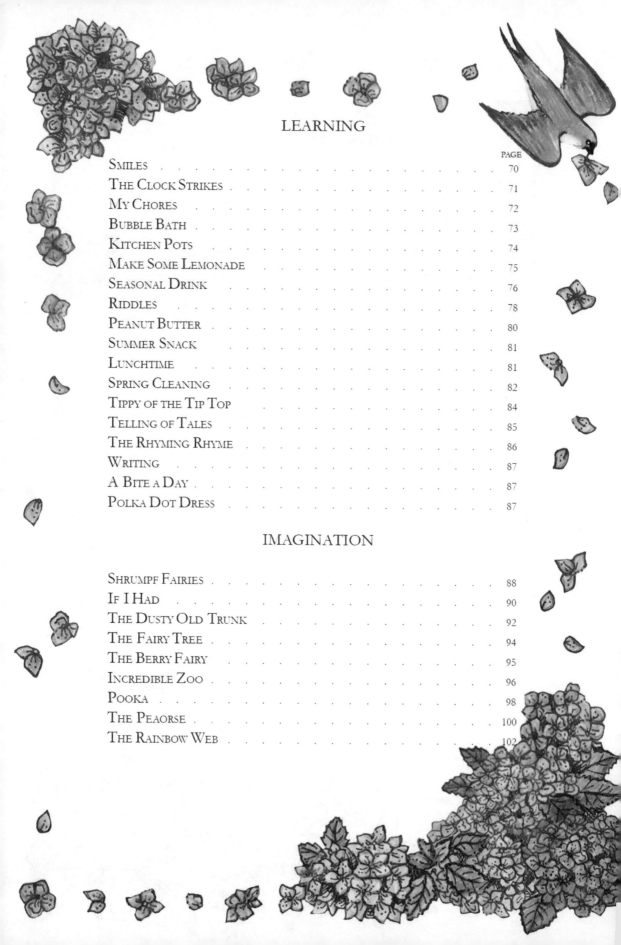

LEARNING

IMAGINATION

A BOOK

A BOOK, a book, come take a look,
To see my very own brand new book!
To discover stories yet untold,
What new journeys are there to behold!
Look inside and you surely will see,
Adventures awaiting just for thee!

ANIMALS ATTIRE

THE Bat in his blue beanie
Makes him look teeny,
Wearing his bitty blue beanie.

The Cat in her crimson coat
Is so swank she likes to gloat,
About her cozy crimson coat.

The Dog in her dotted dress
Likes to dance to impress,
Others with her dotted dress.

The Frog in her fancy frock
Also likes to sit and gawk,
At those without a fancy frock.

The Horse in his heather hood
Can't see where he last stood,
His eyes covered by his heather hood.

The Pig in his purple pants
Likes to garden the green plants,
In his puffy purple pants.

The Rabbit in his red raincoat
Enjoys sailing in his boat,
Keeping dry in his red raincoat.

The Squirrel in her square shoes
Likes to play the Sunday blues,
And tap in her silly square shoes.

The Turkey in his tweed tie
Would like to go and buy,
Another terrific tweed tie.

BEDTIME STORIES

THE evening has passed,
It's bedtime at last.
With my homework done,
Now it's time for some fun!
Time to crawl into bed,
And dream of what I'll be read.
It's rather bright,
I best turn off my overhead light.
When mother comes in,
It means Storytime is about to begin.
Under the covers I go,
To hear stories of long ago.

Ships on the high sea
Are quite adventurous you'll see.
Beneath those vast waters
Lay the story of the singing otters.
I like to listen to the old fable
Of the knights of the round table.
Then there's the tree that is crowned
With pink blossoms year round.
The white church on the hill
Shares its neverending good will.
To hear about the blossoming rainbow
With beautiful blooms all aglow.
It showers its magical powers
With all colorful rainbow flowers.

EVERYDAY DRESS

SEE! Oh do see my everyday dress!
It's the most beautiful amongst all the rest!

First to tell you about my unique dress,
It has a collar like that of a great empress!
It has puffy sleeves like that on a queen,
It's the greatest thing you'll have ever seen!

The tailored bodice is golden brocade,
And my shoes are a soft faux brown suede.
Around my waist I wear a bronze coin belt,
And my cuffs are the fuzziest you've ever felt!

The dress is longer than my own height,
And my petticoat is the color of milk white.
Everything is easy to put together in a pair,
For I have all the colors of the rainbow to wear.

My jeweled necklace sparkles in the light,
And my earrings are an endearing sight!
My headdress is a red foliage bouquet,
It is quite the loveliest thing, I must say!

A hundred different fabrics form the long gown,
See, it's a whole new dress when I turn around!
Around the hem are hundreds of flowers attached,
Everything seems to me to be a perfect match!

WINTER CAROUSEL

COME, come to the Winter Carousel,
Starting off with the sound of a small bell.

Up and down goes the Merry-go-round,
The only one of its kind to be found!

The chilly air turns my cheeks to red,
As snow starts to fall gently overhead.

I shall ride the mighty polar bear,
Or perhaps a sleigh, which we both can share.

There dash the gray wolf and bronze reindeer,
As their riders let out a hearty cheer!

In the mists of the cold winter's night,
Aboard, all colors array, shine out bright.

A countless delight that never ends,
A pure celebration of fun with friends!

THE CHOCOLATE CHIP CAT AND THE LUNA MOTH

THIS cat known as Chip
  Was covered all in white.
Except for all the brown specks,
  That were clear as daylight.

This young chocolate chip cat
  Wasn't like all the others.
She didn't like to hunt,
  Unlike her big brothers.

She didn't quite understand
  Why all night they would chase.
They looked rather quite foolish,
  Running around as if in a race.

Chip preferred to explore
  Through the bushes and trees.
She would ascend and climb,
  Reaching the top with ease.

Through the leaves she went
  And came to see something odd.
Something green with purple tint,
  With stunning wings unflawed.

Chip thought to herself
  How graceful it glides in the sky.
It looks unlike anything I've seen,
  Could it be a long lost butterfly?

"Please don't take my wings!" It cried.
  Chip replied, "Why would I do that?
You must not be scared of me,
  Unlike my brothers, I'm a friendly cat."

"What are you, may I ask?
  For you are the most beautiful of things.
Are you a butterfly of some sorts?
  For you have the loveliest wings."

"I am but a simple Luna Moth
  And need wings just as a cat needs fur."
Chip exclaimed, "Keep your wings,
  I only ask your company", letting out a purr.

So together they played and frolicked
  Throughout the whole of the night.
Without a care in the world,
  They basked until first sunlight.

As those summer nights went by
  They became the closest of friends.
Both had never been happier,
  And that's where our story ends.

MY GREAT CAT

I HAVE a great big jungle cat,
Which compared to the other cats, is rather fat.
He's rather too big to sit on my lap,
So he'll lie outside for a nap.

My pet cat has sharp pointed claws,
And you will not believe the size of his pink paws!
He climbs way up into the woodland trees,
And you best watch out for the fleas!

My pet has big yellow eyes,
And he's always early in the morning to rise.
What a long tongue and mighty teeth he's got,
He's more perfect rather than not.

He has stripes up and down his back,
Decorated in orange with painted lines in black.
My pet is wild and frightening as can be,
So scary that neighbors will flee.

Oh! He is brave but not unkind,
He may be intimidating but don't be blind,
To judge not on one's looks but how one acts.
Those are the true practical facts.

MY PET GIRAFFE

I HAVE a pet giraffe that goes everywhere with me,
He is the neatest pet you will ever dare to see.
He has a great long neck and is covered in brown spots,
He can travel over plains and across parking lots.
He can reach way up high, touching the uppermost house,
And unlike elephants, he isn't scared of a mouse.
We do everything together, you would not believe,
I counted his spots today, at one hundred and three.

THE RED BUFFALO

HAVE you ever seen the Red Buffalo?
They used to roam the trails long ago.
Up they would ascend past the mountain ridge,
There they'd cross any rickety bridge.
They were brave and stronger than a great Ox,
And weighed more than a pile of rocks.

Have you ever seen the Red Buffalo?
Living on the plain green fields below.
They ride in groups of seven, eight or nine,
And eat the barks right off of the pine.
Their frame is nothing but sturdy and thick,
With a hide as tough as a stone brick.

Have you ever seen the Red Buffalo?
You can catch them roaming to and fro.
Galloping from here to there, out of sight.
If they are seen, they are quick to flight.
Don't wander so quickly, take it real slow,
Or you'll miss the red herd on the go.

Your golden moment may just pass you by,
So make sure to keep an open eye.

THE LITTLE OLD COTTAGE

THERE'S a little old cottage,
  Right on the edge of town.
When you see Walden Street,
  Just walk straight on down.
Then take a sharp due left,
  To the edge, then around,
You'll see a rippling stream.

On seeing the rippling stream,
  You'll cross the babbling brook.
Over the bridge to the other side,
  You'll see if you take a look,
A small garden all in bloom,
  All snuggled in a little nook.

Behind that little nook,
  You'll spot it in the grass,
With ivy crawling up its walls,
  And windows made of stain glass.
The outside is made from brick,
  With a roof the color of brass.

Here sits the little old cottage,
  I have finally spotted at last.

THE SILVER SKATES

(Based on the story of *Hans Brinker* Or *The Silver Skates* by Mary Mapes Dodge)

THERE is a contest down one of the frozen lakes.
The first winner receives a pair of silver skates.

I must train hard every day until the race,
To practice long in hopes I can win first place.

But how can I practice, what can I do,
Without a pair of my own skater's shoes?

To gather some leather for the straps,
Along with wood for the skating flats.

They may not work the very best,
But the skates will last nonetheless.

It's early morning, time to rise,
To head where the Canal lies.

Skating till the sun sinks its head,
Now to head home and into bed.

Next day I train till the day is gone,
I'll soon be ready before too long.

The next week it is time for the big race,
I hope I can keep up a good fast pace.

Racing against the frigid December air,
Not sure how much longer my body can bear.

The wind is howling brash and the trees crudely bend,
But I will not give up until the very end!

I pass the finish line almost out of breath,
With my very face and hands as cold as death.

What success! Coming in at silver place,
All distress vanishes from my chill face.

Even with second place I have come so far,
With all of my hard work, I feel like a star.

My beloved friends and family gather around,
To congratulate me on the courage I found.

I am proud of myself for a job well done.
In never giving up, I've already won.

THE LITTLE TRAIN

"CHOO Choo KaDoo!"
The little train spouted.
"I want to explore the world around,
To travel across from town to town!
What a wondrous place, what a sight,
To see it all would be a delight!"

The other trains laughed at the small train,
Saying, "you'll never have ground to gain,
You're far too small to get very far."
With all them laughing, "hardy har har!"

"Choo Choo KaDoo!"
The little train spouted.
"I'm off to a faraway green land,
To travel along the briny sand!
Then across the ocean and the sea,
Wonder how far away it will be?"

The other trains laughed at the small train,
Quoting,"you'll never have ground to gain,
You're far too small to travel so far.
You are not as fast as a motor car!"

"Choo Choo KaDoo!"
The little train spouted.
"I will go through great storms and thick rain,
Each mile more I go I will gain.
Never will I stop when times get tough,
It pays off when the terrain gets rough."

The other trains laughed at the small train,
Stating,"you'll never have ground to gain,
You're far too small to go very far.
Who exactly do you think you are?"

"Choo Choo KaDoo!"
The little train spouted.
He didn't heed and went on ahead,
Leaving behind all his cares and dread.
"Nothing can stop me as I believe,
Once a goal is set, you must achieve."

Off the small train went, starting out slow,
Watching the cliffs up high and below.
There were harsh thunderstorms and cold nights,
Some days the tiny train had such frights.

Still, he continued, his trip in mind,
Not knowing exactly what he would find.
Many miles he traveled and pained,
He kept pushing though his wheels were strained.

Finally, he reached the mountain peaks,
With rushing water within its creeks.
Sites to view beyond any before,
Now to let go to what he had bore.

The sun overhead shined out so bright,
A sight to see beyond his delight.
It was then he grasped, amongst the greens,
That goals can be reached by any means.

The moral of the story is clear to see,
A dream is achievable if you believe.

UP THE PATH

UP the path and down the path, skipping as we go,
Where we will end up going, who will ever know!

Do I see a panther with its eyes glowing bright?
Or perhaps it's a great owl awake in the night.
Will we see an orange tiger or brown bear along the way?
Perhaps see shiny blue minnows swimming along the bay.

Will there be a snake hanging from the jungle top,
Showing its colored stripes, easy for us to spot?
Perhaps I will take a nap with the wild jungle cats,
Or explore the deep hidden caves filled with vampire bats!

Will I see a hundred frogs leaping through the air?
Or perhaps we'll catch sight of a hopping gray hare.
Maybe I'll climb to the tallest branch seated way up high,
To see over the wooden lands and watch the midnight sky.

A sight to perceive, the deer springing to and fro.
To observe their great bounding skills they have to show.
I hope to see some tropical birds way up in the trees,
With red spots and rainbow feathers for everyone to see!

Up the path and down the path, skipping as we go,
Where we will end up going, who will ever know!

WELSH CORGI

HAVE you seen a Welsh Corgi dog,
Whose body is like that of a log?

They have stump legs, along with a bear's tail,
And are short to other dogs when put to scale.

They have great big ears like that of a fox,
And are rather fond of evening walks.

They have a German Shepherd snout,
Though, I am not sure what that's all about.

This may sound unbelievable to you,
But if you saw one you'd know it to be true!

SNOW GOOSE

WITH feathers as smooth as spun silk,
And color, that of fresh cow's milk.

The white goose is such a pretty sight,
With his tail shining in the sunlight.

How did that little goose turn white?
Did he get startled with such fright?

Perhaps he was feeling sick and faint,
Or did he get covered with white paint?

Why, this is no white goose I'm told,
Come see, the Snow Goose to behold!

33

THE PRINCESS AND THE DONKEY

THERE once lived a princess on a green hill
    Whose coming of age they were to celebrate.
To choose her the finest horse at will
    That would be her grandest gift to date.

    The king proclaimed throughout the land
        To find the best for his sweet dear girl,
    And hold a celebration most grand,
        For she was his precious little pearl.

Throughout the kingdom, they did look
    At every stunning stallion and mare.
Over the fields and around every nook,
    Yet nothing suited the princess there.

    Every striking horse, every proud steed,
        Seemed too fixated on their own beauty.
    They would fall short of any good deed,
        And most seemed overly vain and snooty.

Tired with searching, the princess took a walk,
Hiking to the top of the mountain plain.
But hold! her foot got wedged in-between a rock,
Causing her to tumble down the rocky lane.

What a calamity for her to befall,
As she went rolling passed the peak.
Surpassing the drizzling waterfall
And on by the trickling blue creek.

When she awoke, she was lying in the grass,
And as she looked up she saw horses grazing there.
She shouted for help, but they only did pass,
Heeding no notice of the princess in despair.

All alone the princess started to cry,
Not knowing what she could do.
Suddenly she heard a clatter nearby,
Why! it sounded like that of a horseshoe!

What came across was no horse it seemed,
    For he was rather short and stout.
Though his coat didn't shine, his face beamed.
    He then stooped, seeing as she needed helping out.

"You're wondering what I am,
    You need not ask for I shall tell you.
I am a donkey and as gentle as a lamb,
    But strong as an ox when I need to."

She pulled herself onto his great back,
    The donkey then stood and headed down.
His mane was coarse and a coal color black,
    Which everyone noticed as they went through town.

Both were grimy from head to foot,
    And the folks started to gossip around.
Why was the princess covered all in soot,
    And what had happened to her gown?

What caught their eye most of all,
    Was the animal on which she rode.
The donkey gave no notice and standing tall,
    Continued down, passing the main road.

The princess told the donkey to stop,
    And with the help of her dear friend,
She sat up to address the crowd atop,
    Telling them this donkey was a godsend.

"This fellow aided me when others did not,
    And showed me compassion and care.
He gave me more than one could have thought,
    And henceforth shall be my companion everywhere."

From then on they were each other's best friend,
    And though the donkey looked quite plain,
The princess loved him to the very end,
    From his rough hair to his tattered mane.

THE COMBAT

(Inspired by "The Duel" by Eugene Field)

THE orange plaid owl and the batik blue bear
Hadn't known the other was there.
Till one was moved near the other
And soon a duel began with each other.
The yellow kite and the rocking chair
Looked at them scuffle with despair.
Never had such an argument taken place.
(Though I didn't see the combat,
The chair recalled to me their awful spat.)

The orange plaid owl went "Who-o-o!"
And the batik bear gave out a huff too!
The bear growled, and the owl let out a screech,
Soon the ground was laid with bits of each.
While the yellow kite fluttered with dismay,
Each one's anger never did sway.
Such a ruckus was heard throughout the room.
(It is quite a story to behold,
But it's the tale the yellow kite told!)

The rocking chair froze with such fright
For the room was a dreadful sight.
And on and on the two continued their fight
Which never ceased throughout the night.
'T was quarter to three, (so was said)
That neither kite nor chair had gone to bed.
And, oh! how the owl and bear tore about the space!
(This incident I do declare—
As was stated by the rocking chair!)

The next day where they both had sat,
Came to end that awful combat.
Neither was seen ever again
And few recall what happened then.
Many still wonder where the two went;
Some believe it was malcontent.
The truth: each devoured the other.
(The yellow kite spoke it to me,
That is how I know it to be.)

GRANDMOTHER FOX

OH Grandmother Fox in her knitted socks,
Wears a tattered shawl, and glasses that are too small.
A basket she carries filled with delicious blackberries!
She has such clever wit and often goes to sit
Outside in a rocking chair without any care.

Oh Grandmother Fox in her knitted socks,
Can weave such a fantastic story in a flurry.
Stories of far off lands filled with desert sands,
Tales of great riches and peculiar old witches.
Whatever the fable may be, it fills her kits with glee.

Oh Grandmother Fox in her knitted socks,
Teaching among the naïve and the young,
Moral lessons of old that have once been told.
Once her stories are said, she sends the kits to bed,
But not without a berry handful to make them full!

THE WOLF AND CAT

THE two were an unlikely pair,
  If you can believe that…
For this story I'm about to share
  Is about a wolf and his dear cat.

        The wolf, you see, was alone
            And quiet in his own thought.
        If only he had just known
            That his life was to change a lot.

            All the other animals, you see,
                Seemed to be afraid of his kind.
            Not knowing how nice wolves can be,
                They ignored him, paying him no mind.

The wolf wandered here and there,
  One day in search of fresh food.
Not knowing and unaware
  That he was being pursued.

        One soft thump! The wolf turned around,
            Gazing at what hit his foot in surprise.
        It was fuzzy, soft and rather round,
            It was a white cat with great blue eyes!

            The small cat let out a "me-oww!",
                Looking up at the wolf with a grin.
            The lone wolf softened up his brow,
                Lowering down his great chin.

Now if you were to ponder,
  What ever happened to these two,
Well they would forever wander
  Side by side, all the days through.

BENEATH THE OCEAN DEEP

BENEATH the deep, along the ocean floor,
Lies many wondrous beasts to explore.
Some are great, as big as a humpback whale,
While others are too small to put to scale.
There are those that lie hidden in the sand,
While others are able to climb on land.

UP IN THE CLOUDY SKY

IF you look up into the cloudy sky,
You'll see hundreds of birds flying on by.
Sparrows, cardinals, mockingbirds, and blue jays,
Singing out their tune with fluttering praise.
Gliding above like a boat on the sea,
As a bird, never could you feel as free.

ALONG THE GREEN GRASS

WELL along the grassy valley prairie,
Resides a place where the wind is airy.
The early morning sunrise soon reveals,
Flocks of fluffy sheep grazing on the fields.
Quite a blissful setting you'll find below,
There, where the yellow wildflowers grow.

TICK TOCK

TICK tock tick tock there goes the clock,
First strikes at ten then at eleven o'clock.
The clock strikes noon but not too soon.
At one it's time for outdoor fun in the sun!
Tick tock tick tock there goes the clock,
First strikes at two then at three o'clock.
At four people rush to the grocery store,
At five, those from work are yet to arrive.
Tick tock tick tock there goes the clock,
First strikes at six then at seven o'clock.
At eight, time for bed, it's getting late!
At nine the full blue moon is out to shine.
At ten, waiting to do it tomorrow again!

BY THE MOON

B<small>Y</small> the bright starlight
That gleams clearly in sight,
Shining above the vast sky,
The great blue moon floats on by.

Hello there blue moon,
Good to see you so soon.
Where shall we go today,
Perhaps along the byway?

You shall follow me
As softly as can be.
You shall tag right along
As I sing out my sweet song.

"Oh blue moon, how you shine so bright,
Beaming out in the mists of the night.
Softly do you glide right behind,
For those who wander shall seek to find."

"Oh blue moon, how you tail my back,
Seen even when the sky is so black.
Quietly I quicken my pace,
You make haste as if we're in a race."

"Oh blue moon, why are you up high
And only at night do you come by?
See me again my dear old friend,
Do not say this night is at an end."

"Oh blue moon, I will see you soon,
For you are our only one true moon.
Tomorrow's yet another day,
The sun will visit while you're away."

By the bright starlight
That gleams clearly in sight,
Shining above the vast sky,
The great blue moon floats on by.

MY LITTLE GREEN KITE

UP, Up, sways my little green kite,
  Reaching to an incredible height.
Touching the sky in the spring breeze.
Hovering over the tallest of trees.
Further and further, higher it goes,
How far will it reach, nobody knows!

CATTAIL

THIS is no ordinary tale,
  Nor that of a real life feline.
This is a story about the Cattail,
  And their unique tail design.

Cattails grow from the ground
  With their tails up to the sky.
Their ends are tall and round
  And attract the dragonfly.

These tails are rather strong,
  They wag them in the breeze.
Though they are rather long,
  They bend with simple ease.

A keen sight for the eye,
  These tails are soft to touch.
By the ponds do they lie,
  Oh, I do like them so much!

This is no ordinary tale,
  Nor that of a real life cat.
This is a story about the Cattail,
  And let's just leave it at that.

IN THE FOREST BED

LADYBUGS flying quickly overhead,
  Easy to be spotted, covered in red.
Butterflies gather up the road ahead,
While dragonflies buzz over the lakebed.

The crickets play out their violin tune,
As the beetles flick their wings in mid-June.
Water skippers assemble atop the lake,
While amongst the tall grass lies a sly snake.

The wind dances through the towering trees,
As white daisies bow their heads in the breeze.
The colored snails are slow to move along,
As the birds chant out their afternoon song.

To each white flower, the honeybees roam,
Bringing back nectar to their honeycomb.
Reptiles, bugs, and birds live all around,
Giving off their buzz and sweet chirping sound.

KINGDOM OF THE BUGS

THE KING of the jump crickets,
  The queen of the honeybees,
The widow of the black spiders,
  The stinkbugs of the tall trees.
The soldiers of the blue beetles,
  The warriors of the red ants,
Marching long in search of food,
  Whenever they get the chance.

MY LITTLE RAINBOW GARDEN

I HAVE a little rainbow garden that I give tender loving care,
A bountiful collection of vegetables and fruits for me to share.
In my patch of bright colors rests a feast for a king,
A basket of refreshing edibles I shall bring:

One red apple for the sweet juicy taste.
Two orange creamy pumpkins to pick in haste.
Three yellow lemons with sour and zest.
Four green pears always taste the very best.
Five blue blueberries with bitter flesh so sweet.
Six indigo blackberries, such a treat!
Seven violet eggplants ready to eat.

I have a little rainbow garden that I give tender loving care,
A bountiful collection of vegetables and fruits for me to share.
There lays an abundance of brightly colored cuisine,
There, sitting and growing amongst the lush garden's green.

FRUIT SWEETS

PICK-a-pickidy an apple from the apple tree,
To bake a sweet hot pie just for you and me.

Pick-a-pickidy a pear from the pear tree,
Make a delightful treat just for you and me.

Pick-a-pickidy a cherry from the cherry tree,
To cook some tasty tarts just for you and me.

Pick-a-pickidy a pumpkin from the patch,
To make delicious, sweet bread loafs in a batch!

THE JUBILEE OF TREES

SEE the trees all adorned in the colors of the earth,
These wise ancient creations provide their worth.
No tree or sapling is to be left astray
To celebrate the importance of this festive day.

Trees provide us with a great variety of things,
And tells us their age by the number of rings.
An assortment of goods that delivers what we'll need,
They are the ones that provide us with fruit and seed.

Let's see…
There are apple and cherry, plum and pear,
Producing edibles for all to share.
There is the apricot, coconut, and the mango tree,
How much more could there really be?
Well, there are…
Avocado, grapefruit, guava, and pomegranate,
Aren't we lucky to have them on our planet?
Hungry for a snack…
Why not taste an almond or pecan,
Or grab some walnuts and cashews if you can!

Nourishment isn't the only thing trees have to give,
The forest supplies much more for us to live.
Not only do they offer us many things to eat,
They provide us shelter from the sun's harsh heat.

In wintertime, they block out the bitter icy storm,
And provide homes for animals to stay warm.
Trees feed and protect wildlife for them to survive
So many of them can continue to thrive.

Nature, such as trees and plants, produces fresh air,
We should be like them in giving so much care.
Showering us with beauty all along the terrain,
Soak in their earthy scents during the spring rain.

Trees create a majestic backdrop before our eyes,
Its existence itself is our golden prize.
Such a rare treasure we must protect at any cost,
For without them we would certainly be lost.

Have you heard
About the different types of trees,
Like the maple whose leaves are groups of threes?
Giving us delicious syrup to adore,
Which on our pancakes we like to pour.
There is also…
The Sycamore offering up a drinkable sap,
Which birds will try their best to snap.
A hollow within critters have sought,
For in winters, it offers up a cozy spot.
The Great White Oak with its acorn seed,
Offers food for squirrels and deer in need.

The sturdiness of the Chestnut and the Oak
Have provided building supplies for our folk.
Even the golden leaf Birch with their black and white bark
Are more than just a natural forest landmark.

The beautiful Dogwood tree blossoms with white flowers,
As weather brings about its rainy showers.
You're familiar with Evergreens like Cedar and Spruce,
That deliver us with more than just one use.

Who can forget our famous Christmas holiday tree?
Like the White Pine and Fir we all like to see.
Decorated all out in tinsel and yellow lights,
Shining out in the darkness of those cold nights.

Many provide us medical remedies as well,
Within Cherry, Willow, and Elm they do dwell.
It's hard to believe all the things trees have supplied.
We should thank them for everything they provide.

There are much more, though I have just listed a few,
See how important they are to me and you.
Nature has provided the earth with such endless means,
Thus we must try to protect our precious greens.

All trees have a purpose, so treat them with due respect,
Though they're all different, each one is perfect.
Blessed are we to be given a gift of such beauty,
To help preserve these great trees is our duty.

The Jubilee of Trees is but one day in a year,
So bring out your family and your good cheer!
A holiday that should be held above all the rest,
So come celebrate this event at its best!

TRAMPOLINE

JUMP, jump towards the sky,
Let's see how high you can fly!
How far is it you can reach,
Can you see over the hills to the beach?
Can you touch your toes in midair?
Try to do a back flip if you dare!
Can you spring as high as a tree,
Pretending you're a honeybee?
How far up can you go?
Bouncing high then bouncing low.
Jump, jump towards the sky,
Let's see how high you can fly!

BY THE SWING SIDE

COME, come, come! Swing with me by the seaside!
To look out over the great ocean tide!
Like the white seagulls we shall glide,
Over the vast blue waters wide.

Come, come, and see what it is to betide,
To see what the wide world has to provide.
Come, come, come! Swing with me outside!
To swing by me if you decide.

Have you ever reached up so very high,
It feels like you are floating in the sky?
Swing so high you could almost fly,
Watch the clouds as they float on by.

To feel like a red cardinal high in flight,
And be able to soar at such a height!
From way up above, what a sight,
As carefree as a soaring kite!

THE CHERRY TREE

TODAY I planted a small cherry tree,
In hopes of how tall it might grow to be.
I will give it water and nourish it with rich soil,
So my dear friend will never come to spoil.
I wish to see how great it will grow,
Guessing what colors it might have to show.
To speak to my growing tree and give it care,
So it may protect me from the sun's glare.
Love and cherish I shall give my cherry tree,
In hopes of how tall it might grow to be.

BLUEBIRD TREE

HAVE you heard of the beautiful bluebird,
Who has the gold tip wing and loves to sing?
Well, to you I will tell, where they do dwell.
If you're lucky to see the bluebird tree,
There they do swoop and repose in a group.

Looking up above you won't see a dove,
But rather the birds of bright blue, that's who!
You will find a large flock that likes to talk.
They dance in the cool air without a care,
And sing many a sweet tune in mid-June.

Catching a view, you'd see their eggs of blue,
Having lots of stunning speckle gold dots,
But be aware, as they are rather rare,
Their eggs they do keep, buried way down deep,
With their resting place beneath the tree's base.

They chirp quite high, singing to the clear sky,
With their wings of gold, striking to behold.
These birds are quite a sight to see in flight.
Their enchanting songs they sing in a ring,
Unlike any scene you have ever seen.

BY THE GOAT TRAIL

BY and by the little Goat Trail.
I shall grab my bucket and pail,
To walk along the little Goat Trail.

By and by the little Goat Trail.
To start by I must not derail,
To stay beside the little Goat Trail.

By and by the little Goat Trail.
All the summer smells to inhale,
To tread along the little Goat Trail.

By and by the little Goat Trail.
Crossing a sluggish peachy snail,
To stroll beside the little Goat Trail.

By and by the little Goat Trail.
Catching the forest in detail,
To gaze upon the little Goat Trail.

By and by the little Goat Trail.
Spotting a wooden garden rail,
To rest beside the little Goat Trail.

By and by the little Goat Trail.
Gliding by like a ship to sail,
To stride along the little Goat Trail.

By and by the little Goat Trail.
To reach the finish without fail,
To wander by the little Goat Trail.

By and by the little Goat Trail.
Happy little goats swish their tails!
So comes to an end our little Goat Tale.

SPRINGTIME

BIRDS sing out their gayish tune,
   While the sunrays shine out at high noon.
Nature wakes from its long sleep,
While flower buds emerge from the deep.

With a garden to nourish,
A renewed earth begins to flourish.
Stirring at the smell of spring,
Seeing what new life there is to bring.

Bees hum as they go along,
While I sing out a familiar song.
The sun brings warmth to my face,
While hares emerge from their hiding place.

SUMMERTIME

THE sun's warm rays stretch out wide,
What a perfect day to play outside!
White clouds drift in the blue sky
As orange butterflies flutter on by.

To the beach I make a dash,
Down to the sea to make a big splash!
The sand is warm on my feet,
Time for me to find a nice cold treat.

The wind is perfect for flight,
No better time to fly my new kite!
Time to rest now in the grass,
To lay down and have a nap at last.

FALLTIME

THE smell of leaves fills the air,
  As the sun gives off a yellow glare.
Maroon, orange, yellow, and brown,
A quilt of colors brushes the town.

The air is chill down the lane,
And grass is wet from the midnight rain.
Green acorns fall with a crack,
While kids fill the street all dressed in black.

The nightlights are set aglow,
While the corn maze is ready to go.
Harvest is ready to pick,
So better pick your pumpkins real quick!

WINTERTIME

THE northern lights all aglow,
  Over the white hills covered in snow.
  To grab my mittens and sled,
And tread to the mountain up ahead.

The snowflakes start to descend,
As I start to build my snowman friend.
  The crisp cold air smells of pine,
A sweet scent I think is quite divine!

The hearth glows with a fire,
  I scooch in to make myself drier.
  Now to drink some nice hot tea,
Watching the lights twinkle on the tree.

BUTTERFLY PATH

WHAT lay before me but a yellow trail,
 Draped out like a golden silk veil.
The road moves at first glance,
And begins to flutter as I advance.

As I approach the road lifts, breaking apart,
Butterflies scatter, making their depart.
The sky quickly becomes a lemon cloud,
Covered in a thick saffron shroud.

Butterflies, butterflies every which way!
They flurry and dance as if in a ballet.
Flashes of yellow cream-colored wings,
What beauty compared to all other things!

AIRWAY TO INDIA

THE SMELL of spices fills the air,
With folks rushing from here to there.
The monkeys clatter from up above,
Trying to see what food they can snub.
A palette of bright colors paints the street.
A dish filled with various things to eat.
Taste the freshly caught fish from the sea,
Accompanied by a side of tea.
Children playing cricket in the lane,
While a rush of folks boards the train.
Temples shine in the bustling town,
Draped with flower garlands all around.
The honking of cars as they drive on by,
While bright fireworks fill the evening sky.
Monsoon floods fill the alleyway,
While houseboats float on down by the bay.
Donkeys take on a heavy load,
As Gir cows tread down the packed road.
Rickshaws zoom on by, tooting a tune,
Rushing passed in the late afternoon.
Waterfalls trickle down the steep mountains,
Sprinkling the earth like water fountains.
A tapestry of art to each dress.
A time of prayers and a life to bless.
City lights give a warming glow,
A magical sight to bestow.

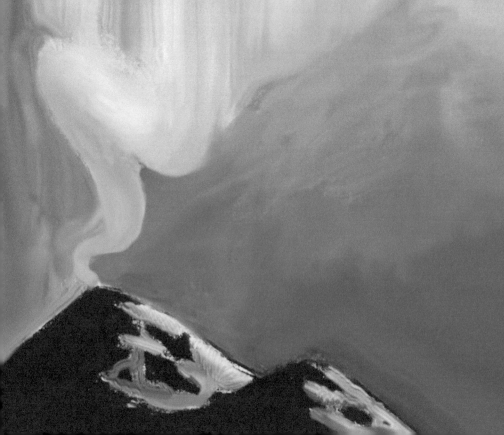

NORTHERN LIGHTS

WAY up to the north,
  Where nature calls forth,
Lies a still frozen land.

In the cold dark nights,
Amidst the star lights,
Lays the great beyond.

Gliding up overhead,
Reflecting over the lakebed,
A palette sails across.

Gliding across the sky,
The Aurora streaks on by,
Dancing a spectacle of color.

THE THUNDERSTORM

CRACK with a bright flash, boom with a shake,
Noise so piercing it makes the earth quake.
The sky lights up as if it were twelve noon,
But the bright light once lit ends all too soon.
Dark clouds accumulate, all gather around,
To look below and see what is to be found.

Bang like a drum, rumble like a growl,
The wind gives off a deafening howl.
The moaning gust is flurrying outside,
With noise so loud I want to go and hide.
The rain clouds give out a deep grumbling sound,
As a striking explosion hits the damp ground.

Clatter of a clap, blast of a light,
Shaking the ground with all of its might.
A flurry of a breeze bites at my back,
As the thunder rolls by with a din clack.
The darkening shadows of the cloudy sky,
Let through a crackle, a deaf defying cry.

SMILES

I LIKE to smile to you,
I like to smile to me,
I like to smile at everyone,
  To all those that I see.

Smiles are spread all around
  So you best better beware!
Or you will catch the smiling bug,
  With or without a care.

Smiles are very catchy,
  Like a cold on a chill day.
You better be careful and watch out!
  That's the one thing I'll say.

THE CLOCK STRIKES

DING! Ding! Ding! Ding! Ding! Ding! Ding! Ding!
The clock strikes eight, time to wake before it's too late!
Ding! Ding! Ding! Ding! Ding! Ding! Ding! Ding! Ding!
The clock strikes nine, all head to the hall to dine in line.
Ding! Ding! Ding! Ding! Ding! Ding! Ding! Ding! Ding! Ding!
The clock strikes ten, time to feed the hen in the pen.
Ding! Ding! Ding! Ding! Ding! Ding! Ding! Ding! Ding! Ding! Ding!
The clock strikes eleven with Kevin almost seven!
Ding! Ding! Ding! Ding! Ding! Ding! Ding! Ding! Ding! Ding! Ding! Ding!
The clock strikes noon in June as I sing a merry tune.
Ding!
The clock strikes one, to the field to run in the sun!
Ding! Ding!
The clock strikes two, as the new cows in the meadow moo.
Ding! Ding! Ding!
The clock strikes three, time for me to climb a tree!
Ding! Ding! Ding! Ding!
The clock strikes four, time for my chore to fix the broken door.
Ding! Ding! Ding! Ding! Ding!
The clock strikes five, I arrive at the pond to dive!
Ding! Ding! Ding! Ding! Ding! Ding!
The clock strikes six, now to mix some mortar to lay bricks.
Ding! Ding! Ding! Ding! Ding! Ding! Ding!
The clock strikes seven, as Evan looks at heaven.
Ding! Ding! Ding! Ding! Ding! Ding! Ding! Ding!
The clock strikes eight, to head straight home before it's too late.

MY CHORES

TODAY is chore day, time to clean!
Time to sweep up the dirt and dust off the screen.

To mop up the filth on the floor,
That is certainly not a tough cleaning chore.

What grime, what filth to be seen,
Better get all nooks and crannies in between!

Time to polish up the front door,
And clean out all the clutter in my top drawer.

Now to put all my toys away,
I'll set up décor in a lovely array.

Now to play outside in the green,
For everything now is all spotless and clean!

BUBBLE BATH

BUBBLES, bubbles in my tub,
Time I need a good clean scrub!

Some are big while others are small,
And take the shape of a baseball.

Pop those clear rainbow globes in midair,
Some alone and others in a pair.

Light as a feather and white like the snow,
Let's see how big a circle I can blow!

Let's see how high I can stack them on my head,
Or perhaps put on a bubble beard instead.

Flurry away my little bubble friends,
Time for me to finish my evening cleanse.

Ah! The smell of a fresh blossomed rose.
What a wondrous sense to my nose.

Pop, pop, pop, pop! There they all go!
Before they land on down below.

Hear that crispy foamy sound,
As bubbles float all around.

KITCHEN POTS

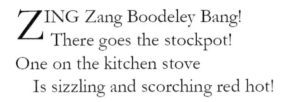

ZING Zang Boodeley Bang!
  There goes the stockpot!
One on the kitchen stove
  Is sizzling and scorching red hot!

Bing Bunk Zippity Zop!
  They will soon all drop!
The kettle's whistling
  While the bubbling won't cease to stop!

Zig Zag Biggily Bag!
  What a messy slop!
The pan is boiling
  And about to fall with one great plop!

Crick Crack Dippity Dop!
  It's burning on top!
The cooker is roasting
  And no doubt the hotplate will go pop!

Bip Bop Tippery Top!
  That's one thing I got!
To turn off the hot stove
  Because it's overflowing a lot!

MAKE SOME LEMONADE

LEMONADE, Lemonade, is what I shall make on such a day!

> First, three ingredients I will need:
> 6 yellow lemons (what a treat!)
> 1 cup white sugar (oh so sweet!)
> 6 cups cold water (to beat the heat!)

First, to squeeze all we can from the lemons to make one cup juice.
Next, I will grab a gallon pitcher, that will be of much use!
Now add the sugar and water to the juice in our pitcher.
That will certainly make our lemonade taste a lot richer!

Last, but surely not in the least, or so I've been told,
Is to add a few ice cubes to keep it nice and cold!

SEASONAL DRINK

SO approaches the season of spring,
Oh, what joyous weather it will bring!
I'm ready for my seasonal drink,
Something quite refreshing I should think.

What will be best to quench my thirst?
Perhaps some lemonade at first!
Bitter sweetness to my pink lips,
Now I'm real hungry for some chips!

Now approaches the season of summer,
If it ends too soon, that'll be a bummer!
Now for the seasonal drink of my choice,
"A fruit smoothie to go!" I say in rejoice.

Smooth and cold, how thirsty I must be,
As I soak in the sun by the sea.
On such a day there's nothing to beat,
Than quenching your thirst with such a treat!

Here approaches the season of fall,
Time to grab my coat and my warm shawl!
With the array of colors outside,
I feel like a warm drink and hayride!

With the apple trees flourishing,
Empty bellies they're nourishing,
"Apple cider is what I'd love,"
There's nothing better to speak of.

Thus approaches the cold winter season,
Don't ask me, for I don't know the reason.
Bitterly cold as the icy breeze blows,
I need a hot drink for my feet just froze!

A nice hot chocolate, and just a hint
Of the sweet taste of a peppermint!
A few marshmallows to top my drink,
Then I'm off to skate at the ice rink!

YOU see things clearly,
You mimic all that I do.
When you see me I see you.
Mirror

I CAN'T be seen in the day,
But at sunset do I fly.
Glowing with a yellow light,
Yet I shine only at night.
Firefly

I HAVE but one hand to hold
And drink much more than I weigh.
When I bow I make it rain,
Bringing green to the terrain.
Watering Can

G LIDING on my belly,
Without limbs I get around,
Under rocks is where I'm found.
A Snake

W RAPPED in an embrace,
Warmth to you I bring,
You shed me come spring.
A coat

I HAVE two fast legs,
But cannot stand alone,
Unless you sit upon my throne.
A Bike

H AND in hand I glide,
Traveling by air,
To show how much I care.
Letter

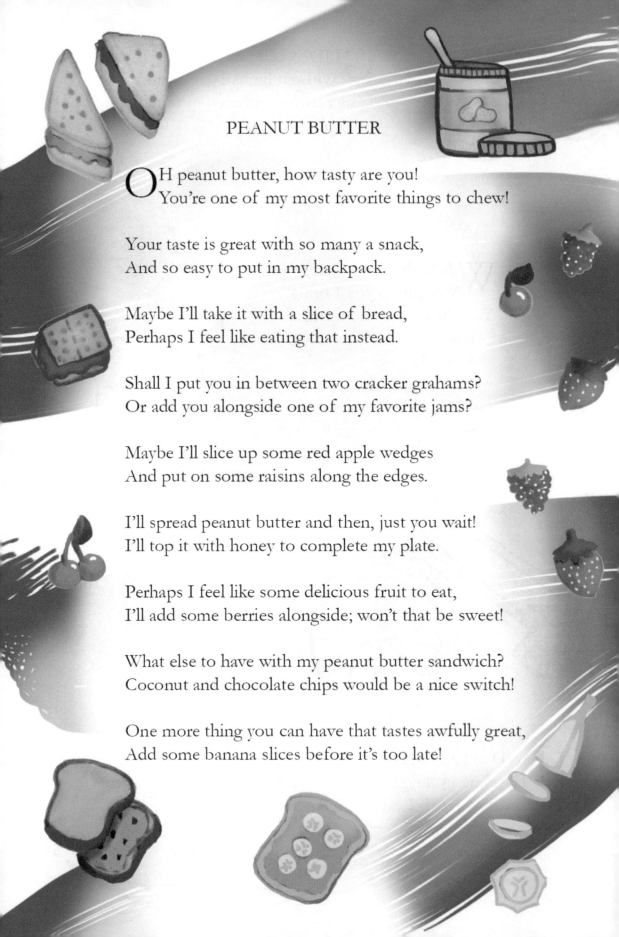

PEANUT BUTTER

OH peanut butter, how tasty are you!
You're one of my most favorite things to chew!

Your taste is great with so many a snack,
And so easy to put in my backpack.

Maybe I'll take it with a slice of bread,
Perhaps I feel like eating that instead.

Shall I put you in between two cracker grahams?
Or add you alongside one of my favorite jams?

Maybe I'll slice up some red apple wedges
And put on some raisins along the edges.

I'll spread peanut butter and then, just you wait!
I'll top it with honey to complete my plate.

Perhaps I feel like some delicious fruit to eat,
I'll add some berries alongside; won't that be sweet!

What else to have with my peanut butter sandwich?
Coconut and chocolate chips would be a nice switch!

One more thing you can have that tastes awfully great,
Add some banana slices before it's too late!

SUMMER SNACK

TIME for a sweet salad, but not of the green kind.
This is where we grab different fruits to be combined.
A delectable fruit salad is what we'll whip up.
Slice up a peach, along with blueberries; just a cup.
Next, dice up a banana, an apple and pear,
Along with some grapes if you have any to spare.
Now, to top it with vanilla yogurt for flavor.
Mix it all in and you have quite a taste to savor!

LUNCHTIME

"WHAT to bake? Or rather, something to make…
Perhaps a loaf of bread? No; best make a sandwich instead."

I'll grab two pieces of whole wheat; "now, what else shall I eat?"
I mutter, "Where is the peanut butter?"

"Ah ha! Here it is!" Found it on the shelf all by myself.
Now for some strawberry jelly to complete my deli.

"A PB&J just for me. My favorite lunch food I must agree!"

SPRING CLEANING

SPRING is finally here, time for something new!
There looks to be so much mess, I'll need a clean up crew!

I'll need to vacuum the floor then dust my wooden desk,
There's something in the corner that looks awfully grotesque!

There's a mountain of toys awaiting me in the closet,
I better make a pile for a donation deposit.

I found a pair of socks, well…there's more than a few.
I own a bouncy ball and jump rope, who knew?

Now to polish my dresser and stand,
Soon my room will look shiny and grand!

Do you think I'll find some games under my bed?
Nope, it seems to be just dust bunnies instead.

Organizing the books on my shelf,
Can you believe I did it all by myself?

I want to rearrange my furniture around the room,
And sweep up any spots I missed with a broom.

All done, doesn't it look great,
Compared to the state it was in at any rate?

I really don't need so many things, this really was a mess.
I should only have a few, for as they say, "more is less".

TIPPY OF THE TIP TOP

TIPPY of the Tip Top
Sits amidst the tall trees.
Moving from forest to forest,
Removing anything unfit he sees.

Tippy of the Tip Top
Likes to keep nature clean.
He helps animals when in need,
And keeps our fields lush and green.

Tippy of the Tip Top
Is the collector of what we waste.
When he spots litter, he removes it,
Picking up trash others have placed.

Tippy of the Tip Top
Gathers what's been left behind.
He takes what we toss outside,
And recycles what he might find.

Tippy of the Tip Top
Puts away what we throw,
To the proper disposal place,
So the Earth can continue to grow.

TELLING OF TALES

MANY tales and stories have been told,
Some tellings brand new, some very old.
There are those with a moral lesson to learn,
And those that will fill you with fright and concern.
They can make you imagine beyond reality,
Or fill your heart with remorse and bitter tragedy.

Countless trips journeyed and combats won,
Adventures strenuous, others fun.
Battling a dark knight or mad evil king,
Reading further on, in what hopes it may bring.
To be told a tale or be Teller of Tales,
Make sure to never pass up on the crucial details.

Legends, myths, books, fables and tall tales,
A road that takes you down many trails.
The mind creates a world of its very own,
Each page is learning about what's yet unknown.
What shall I experience today you may well ask?
Why don't you turn the next page, if you're up for the task!

THE RHYMING RHYME

HAVE you ever heard of the rhyming rhyme?
It keeps in sync beat as well as good time.
Many stories of poems have gone around,
But not so tightly a rhyme has been found.

You can try your skill at ABAB,
Or other styles if you care to see.
In going along with AABB,
Which I prefer, if you wish to agree.
Then there is the way of ABCB.
Which is not the exact style for me.
Or try your hand at ABAAB,
For authors this is ideally the key.
Perhaps attempt AABBCC,
Some say that is how all poems ought to be.

Rhyming the rhymes in every which way,
New means continue to grow to this day.
Now you have completed the rhyming rhyme,
It's quite the thing to pass away the time!

WRITING

WHAT oh what shall I ever write about?
There are so many ideas I've no doubt!
Possibly a novel of my own choice,
That would certainly capture my true voice.

There are so many ideas to be had,
Romantic, heroic, happy, and sad.
Well, perhaps my ideas can surely wait,
I should get to bed, for it's nearly eight!

A BITE A DAY

"AN apple a day keeps the doctor away",
Or so, that's what I have been told.
So I eat away at my apple all day,
In hopes I don't catch a cold!

POLKA DOT DRESS

ONE dot
Two dot
Three dot
Four
When you're ready, I'll count out some more.
Five dot
Six dot
Seven dot
Eight
I'll soon reach a hundred at any rate.

SHRUMPF FAIRIES

HAVE you ever heard of a Shrumpf fairy?
　　For they are not easy to spot.
They often are found along a prairie,
　　And they are not ones to be caught.

The Shrumpfs don't look like other fairies do.
　　For most, they may cause quite a fright!
For if found, you would know it to be true,
　　They're quite a bewildering sight!

Don't be mistaken though, for they're not mean,
　　They are actually quite merry.
Though, if they're unfortunate to be seen,
　　They may be immensely scary.

Their wings resemble a white mushroom cap,
    And their figures, a sleek pale form.
They are surely impossible to entrap,
    For most can easily transform.

They dance amongst the mossy green,
    When the forest is quiet at twilight.
If they're in need to flee the scene,
    The Shrumpf fairies will simply take on flight.

These fairies haven't been seen forever,
    But are not soon to be forgot.
These mystical creatures are quite clever,
    Especially those that are sought.

IF I HAD

IF I had wings I would fly,
  Fly up high into the sky.
Soaring down and swooping low,
Gliding around to and fro.

If I had a monkey's tail,
Through the branches I would sail.
Swinging high while upside down,
Acting like a silly clown.

If I slithered like a snake,
What a hissing I would make!
With my long tongue and thick scales,
I would glide along the trails.

If I had a nose like a dog,
I could sniff through any dense smog.
How I could track down anything,
What many great finds I would bring.

If I had eyes like a great hawk,
I'd hover over the sea dock.
To try and catch a tasty fish,
That would be my only true wish.

If I had such massive sharp claws,
Resting on my giant pink paws,
I could climb the greatest of trees,
And nap in the cool midnight breeze.

If I had ears like that of a cat,
What would my family think of that!
Far and wide, what is it I might hear?
Overhear from my very sharp ear.

If I had teeth like that of a bear,
How it would put others in a scare!
With such big fangs can cause a real fright,
Especially in the dark midnight.

If I had a neck like a giraffe,
How the people would stand up and laugh.
To see movies without being blocked,
The neighbors would certainly be shocked.

If I was a lion with a great roar,
The noise could blow down any mighty door.
Others would cower by such a holler,
I would need to wear a muzzle collar.

If I could jump high like a kangaroo,
Can you imagine the things I could do?
To bounce up high and see all that's around,
To have my own feet lift right off the ground!

If I had gills I would swim in the deep,
Jumping in the water with one great leap.
Deep in the ocean along the sea bed,
Seeing what there is to see on ahead.

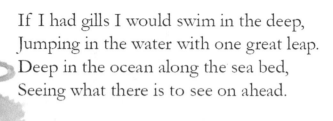

91

THE DUSTY OLD TRUNK

THERE is a great big trunk,
That sits on a musty bunk,
In the attic way up high,
With cobwebs at its side.
What lies inside to behold?
Maybe rubies or real gold.

What great fun, what a delight!
What splendid things to grasp on sight!
To open this trunk is my plan,
To find a way if I can.
Grasp and pull as hard as I might,
Maybe if I clasp it just right.

Peek inside and what do I see,
Historical riches now let free.
What for a wondrous thing to view,
Whose are they, I haven't a clue.
Vintage hats, shoes, costumes, and much more;
Objects as old as the civil war.

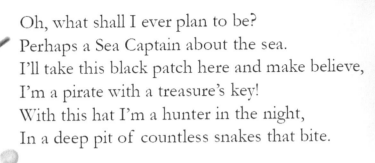

Oh, what shall I ever plan to be?
Perhaps a Sea Captain about the sea.
I'll take this black patch here and make believe,
I'm a pirate with a treasure's key!
With this hat I'm a hunter in the night,
In a deep pit of countless snakes that bite.

With this cape I can fly around,
And save a city with one great bound!
Look what I found, an old baseball glove,
I'll catch a fly ball from above!
I'm a detective with this flashlight,
Catching any robbers taking flight.

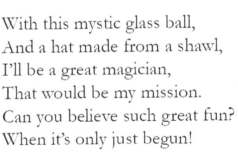

I'll put on this scuba gear,
To dive deep without any fear.
To search for something very old,
To discover some lost gold.
With this blanket I'll be a bear,
It shall be my own fur to wear.

With this mystic glass ball,
And a hat made from a shawl,
I'll be a great magician,
That would be my mission.
Can you believe such great fun?
When it's only just begun!

THE FAIRY TREE

QUIET now as you sneak around the Fairy Tree.
There are many different fairies you can spot.
If you keep still, you might just come to see,
    Just try and make sure you are not caught!

So tread softly as you approach the Fairy Tree,
    To sneak about and look what is to be found.
Little fairies with faces all aglee,
    With hand in hand, dancing all around.

Be still, as you come and behold the Fairy Tree.
    Within lies a glimmer, twinkling aglow.
Quickly make haste, as they are sure to flee,
    To see what magic they have to show.

THE BERRY FAIRY

UNLIKE the fairies you well know,
   These types of fairies are unusual.
They are not dandy or all aglow,
   Nor shine like a ruby red jewel.

These fairies are not too bright,
   Only when it comes to a berry,
Then they have quite the appetite,
   And take on more than they can carry.

Their bellies are fairly plump,
   Like a berry, they are round.
Though big, they can jump
   Tree to tree without a sound.

The berry fairy can blend in well,
   Looking just like another berry.
Deep in the bushes they do dwell,
   Much like any other fairy.

They collect all they can
   For the coming wintertime.
Nothing's more important than
   Storing enough till springtime.

Once again they are all out,
   Starving for the next berry.
Making their way, flying all about,
   Perhaps to snag a nice red cherry!

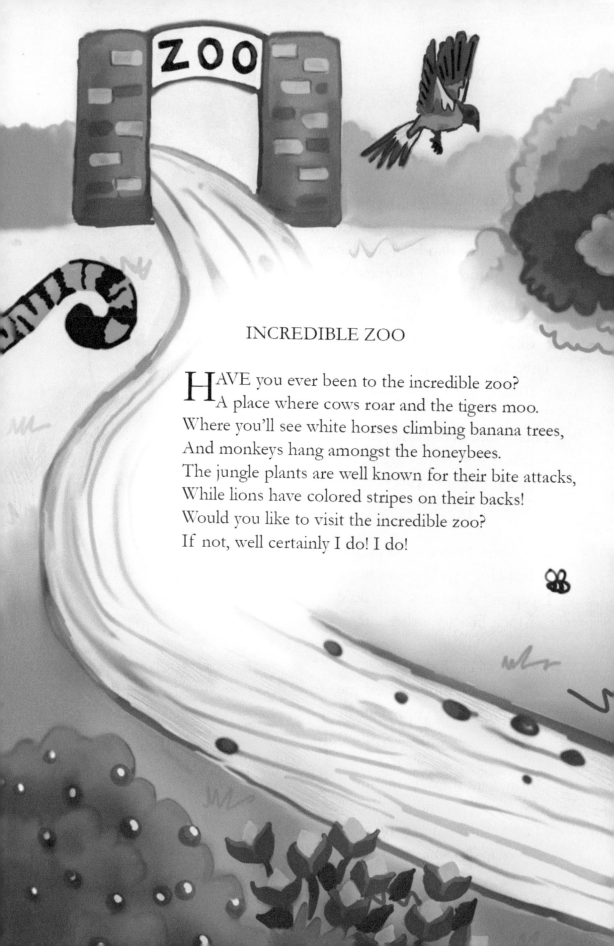

INCREDIBLE ZOO

HAVE you ever been to the incredible zoo?
A place where cows roar and the tigers moo.
Where you'll see white horses climbing banana trees,
And monkeys hang amongst the honeybees.
The jungle plants are well known for their bite attacks,
While lions have colored stripes on their backs!
Would you like to visit the incredible zoo?
If not, well certainly I do! I do!

POOKA

A POOKA.

Have you ever heard of such a strange word?
In tales of folklore in days of yore,
From the Celtic tale we will soon unveil,
The legend of old I will now unfold.

A Pooka.
Seen only to a select few, if you only knew.
I should also inform, that it takes animal form,
Often as a goat, horse, or rabbit out of habit.
They may appear rather large, and can surely take charge.

A Pooka.
There are beings that have proclaimed that this is so named,
That one should be wary towards this creature like fairy.
They're a mystery even with their long history,
Doers of bad or good, depending on where you stood.

A Pooka.
They can be merry, but to mean people, they're scary.
For a wicked person, you see, their luck would worsen.
For those who are not very nice certainly pay the price.
So best be good so your behavior is understood.

A Pooka.
For if your goal is to be an honorable soul,
Then a Pooka indubitably brings good luck things.
Playful but wise, whenever needed they will arise.
Though tricky in their own ways, they'll stick with you always.

A Pooka.
Mischievous by design, though benign,
They may appear here or may appear there.
Seen now and then, and sometimes once again,
So if you're about, be on the lookout.

THE PEAORSE

IN the mystic lands of Shubblelee,
There you will not believe what you see.
In a long forgotten clove within a grassland
Lies a magical creature that is rather grand.

You must have a quick ear and a sharp eye,
If ever you are to see this animal tread on by.
Unknown to our world, this spirit is hard to spot,
Rarest of sights humans have ever caught.

Rather like a peacock and a horse,
This creature is known as a Peaorse.
It graces and floats across the cool grass,
A sight that one should not surpass.

Velvet tallulaberries are its favorite treat,
With its juicy center, they are quite sweet!
The Peaorse takes rest in the bright of day,
But when night falls, it comes out to play.

Its tail with a thousand feathers shines out bright,
Twinkling its colors in the deep moonlight.
There they gallop across the dewdrop ground,
Sprinting here to there without a sound.

I've been told they're shy but noble creatures,
Slender and tall with such elegant features.
If you are fortunate enough to see such a sight,
Like me, you'd want your own Peaorse story to write!

THE RAINBOW WEB

OH, where does the rainbow web come from?
  Glittering in the light of day?
See how beautiful it has become,
  Arranged like a floral bouquet!

Oh, where does the rainbow web come from?
  For the web is a sturdy force.
It may stump a few, even some,
  For it's the rainbow spider of course!